FLOODED WORLD

FLOODED WORLD

Eve Ainsworth

Illustrated by
Carl Pearce

Collins

Chapter 1

I woke to his singing again last night. Soft but still broken, his voice chipped against the cold breeze. It was a song I recognised. One he had whispered to me many times before when I'd been too cold and scared to move. When I truly thought the end was coming.

No tears now, not now sweet one

The stars are here, the night has come

We wait for dark, we wait to sleep

An endless rest. No need to weep.

I sat up. He was standing at the front of the boat, his hands clutching his cloak tightly against his chest. His hair, long and wild, was whipping in the wind. He seemed shorter somehow which was impossible I know, but I could see the sharp outlines of his arms, bony and frail. He wasn't eating enough. He was barely the same man who had boarded this boat all those months ago; how many exactly I don't know as I've lost count.

I watched as his head tipped back and his soft laughter filled the air.

"Dad," I whispered. But I knew he would not turn. He was lost to me.

His laughter had once been a joyful thing – something that meant good things were about to happen, but now it tore through me like a knife. His laugh was a taunt, a mockery at the plight we found ourselves in.

And there was no turning back.

The fact is, living on this boat is hard. There's no escape, nowhere to run and there's a constant fear that we might not make it, but we had no other choice. We had to flee the lands or allow them to destroy us forever. The little land that's left behind is not as it once was. It's diseased and broken now. It has barely survived the Storm Years.

Dad says there's a new future for us. He knows of the safe lands, within the Alps. Friends we know have gone there before us.

And now, finally, it's our turn to join them.

First light. I wake again, stiff and sore. I stretch out my limbs and bite my lip as the pain drills down into my muscle. My bones feel like they will break. It's getting much colder now. Dad says the nights are drawing in. More long, chilled hours trapped aboard this rotting boat. Another struggle for us fighting against a harsh winter.

Us.

But not "Us" at all.

I.

Because this time I'm more or less on my own.

I'm not sure, because we can never be sure of exact dates, but I think today might be my fourteenth birthday. I'm not even sure how I feel about this. Having a birthday on this bleak, small boat was never going to be fun but daring to think of my birthdays in the past just hurts too much.

I have to try and forget instead.

Dad's huddled across the boat from me in a tight ball. His cloak is now drawn like a blanket over his dark clothes. His white, skeletal face is tipped forward. I stagger up, moving unsteadily with the slow movements of the boat. As I draw closer to Dad, I can hear his breath, more ragged now, just painful snatches of air really. I long to pull the wind from the sky and fill his lungs with pure, sweet breeze – but I know it'll do no good. Dad is sinking. We should've slept inside last night. We were foolish. Too busy looking at the stars. Too busy dreaming.

"Just imagine – just imagine how many of those distant stars have already burnt out, Son? So much death already in this universe. To us they sparkle – but we're seeing an old image, something from the past. A reminder that life was once good. So much was alive – "

I shouldn't have let him stay out so long. He already had the beginnings of a cold and now it's much, much worse.

I nudge his shoulder, and he groans softly. His body shifts and then slowly an eye opens – grey and bloodshot. It closes again. Another groan and he pushes his cloak away. His gaze refocuses. He can finally see me. I see the tears pool in his eyes. I watch as he bites his lip, forcing back another groan as he shifts into a seated position.

"Jack? Is it late?"

"The sun is rising. You need to eat."

"Save it. You need to save it for yourself. For Jenna."

I ignore him, as I have done for the past few days. I make my way to the small hold. It's filled with jars of food that Dad stocked here for so long, painstakingly keeping food and provisions by to ensure we had enough for this journey.

Along one side of the cabin are our tools, food, cleaning materials, blankets. The knife. Our toilet, which is curtained off from the rest. Along the other side is one bunk bed that we sleep in. Jenna and I top to tail on the top bunk, and Dad's on the bottom bunk, except lately he's been sleeping on the floor, his blanket whipped tightly across him. He fears his sickness is catching; I know he fears that it's something worse. We each haven't taken much from home as there's so little room. A few books are stacked behind the bed. Some photos are safely stored in our pillows, and Jenna has one doll, Lola, that she clings to for dear life. It's not much of a home – but it's ours and it's kept us alive, so far.

I try to ignore my worries about Dad and focus on cooking instead. Jenna's on the bed, singing softly to Lola. She has a sweet voice. Dad says it's like Mum's and that makes my heart crack open a little more. I don't tell Dad that I can barely remember Mum, that her face is slipping away from me like clouds in the sky. I don't want to upset him any more.

It's tomato soup today. Cold and straight from the jar. It tastes metallic. It tastes like the blood in my mouth when I bite my tongue too hard.

But it's OK. I'm always hungry. The emptiness inside me never really goes. Food, what little we have of it, is a small blessing, so I try to be grateful.

Jenna has a little first, tipping the red sweet liquid straight into her mouth. Then it's Dad's turn. He doesn't resist as I pass the jar to him. He groans

a little, but he still drinks. Red flecks get caught in his beard and he doesn't bother to wipe it away. There is a bit left for me and I take it hungrily, trying not to guzzle too fast.

"I watched and waited all night," Dad says, his eyes as cold as flint. "The sea was still. Empty."

I wish that I could feel relief about that, but we both know that means nothing. The Ravangers are fast and fearless. It's as if they don't need sleep at all. They feed off our weaknesses.

"You really need to eat more," I say. "You can't do this if you don't keep your energy up."

"You shouldn't worry about me, Son."

But I do, Dad, I do.

I can't remember a time when I haven't.

Chapter 2

The day is passing slowly, and Dad's still sleeping. I've managed to keep the ship stable. The winds are calm, and we're heading in the right direction, or at least I hope we are. All I have for reference are some old sea maps, a rusty compass and the sun and stars to guide us.

Jenna is unsettled and who can blame her? She spent her eighth birthday on this boat and I can't tell her how much longer we will be travelling. I watch as she sits on the bed, whispering to Lola, her dark eyes assessing Dad. I can see the worry on her face. She was only young when Mum was taken, but she knows the stories. She knows only too well that sickness is a curse that hangs like a heavy cloud over all of us.

All we can do is hope that Dad's is a passing illness, perhaps a fever caught from sleeping too long in the cold or from not eating properly.

We hope that it's not The Plague.

I comfort Jenna by telling her stories. Sometimes we read together. One book is a battered collection of fairy stories that was once mine, and our mother's before that. Jenna loves stories about princesses and faraway castles. It's

a world that she can't imagine, and neither can I any more.

I tell her about home, about life before The Plague and sometimes, if I'm not too tired, I tell her what I know about life before the floods, before the Storm Years.

Home was a different place then, far west from here. If I squeeze my eyes tightly shut, I can still see it. Our tiny houses built on the edges of the large hillside. The burning fire-pit. The deep, thick woods.

Our village was called Novum – which Dad told me meant The New Beginning.

I can't recall an earliest memory, not an exact one anyway. Everything seems to merge into one now in my mind. I remember the warmth of the large campfire as we all settled around it with the other villagers, cooking food and singing songs. I can still smell the scent of ash and fatty meat cooking. And there was always noise, so much noise. Chatter, shouts, laughter. Dad used to say that you could never escape from the sounds or sights of another villager. That's what happened after the

flooding. Those that survived banded close together, desperate to rebuild and restore what was left of the battered communities.

At least that's what some people did. I don't tell Jenna about the people who looted and stole food. The rumours are those same wandering souls sail large ships at night, looking for weaker vessels that they can hunt and take provisions from. Dad calls them the Ravangers. They are the thieves of the sea.

I don't tell Jenna any of this because it scares me enough. She doesn't need to hear it too.

I think the noise is what I miss the most. The silence now cuts through me. I long to be back in Novum again, my hands clamped to my ears complaining about the loudness, my skin hot from sitting too near that fire, my back aching from cutting wood all day long.

Once I thought that it was the worst way to live. Now I want to be there more than anything else. I dream of turning this boat around and going back.

Except we can't. Tears bite my eyes as I remember this. There's no going back now. The Plague took nearly all of us. We had to escape. It was the only way.

I think of our house; it was at the end

of the small track. Rebuilt from a cottage that once stood there years ago from the days before the floods. Dad said our grandad had restored it as best he could. There was just a small kitchen and living area and two bedrooms above. Once there had been lights in there and heating – I couldn't even begin to imagine that. But we were lucky that there were fireplaces in every room – not everyone had that. Mum found old sacks and cloths that we could sleep on. Huddled together, we were never too cold.

I remember Tim and his family. They lived in the cave at the bottom of the village. In the damp and the rot. It was no wonder that The Plague took them first. No wonder they were the first to go.

We would sit around the fire at night and tell stories to one another. We'd sing and provide comfort. The Elders – Dad, Malc and Annie – would talk the most. They would tell tales from the world before. How the sea used to be contained and how entire areas of land were free to roam. This was long before the sea became angered and rose. Then, millions lived freely. I would sit alongside Elise, my best friend. She would squeeze my hand until my skin turned numb. She would whisper in my ear.

"We don't need to worry about this. We have this now. Our home. Who needs the past?"

These tales from before seemed like fantasy stories, like something from a dream – but there were still books in the village, pictures, items from before that had been salvaged and stored. They showed

us what the world had been like. The creatures that had existed once. The world as it was before the sea took over. And the world before The Plague ruled us all.

Now, what's left of us hide away in the mountains, fighting an illness that no one seems to know the cure for, or risk their lives out in the deep, dark water in the hope that there's something better out there. The water that had claimed so many before us.

There is no other way.

I don't tell Jenna any of this. I focus on the campfires, the happy songs and the friendships that were made. I sketch the mountain range in the dust on the wooden boards and point between the peaks. "There we'll be happy again," I whisper. "There is where everything will return to normal."

But I know in my heart this can never happen. All I want is Mum back, cured and strong, her arms ready to hold us and her eyes filled with love, and I know that's not possible.

I still think of Elise in the long, dark nights.

I think of her huge eyes, dark like mine but brimming with tears, when I told her we were finally leaving. It was late at night, but her skin was still hot to touch. Her cough was dry and racking. Her fingers were like tiny bones in my hand. I knew she was scared and that was the worst thing of all. Guilt rooted me to the spot, despite Dad's shouts to hurry up.

I still think of her. I wonder how long it took for The Plague to take her. I hope she didn't suffer long and that in the end it was painless. But most of all I hope that she forgave me for leaving.

Chapter 3

Dad's still very sick. He's spent another night restless and crying out. Sometimes his words make no sense at all, but sometimes he calls for Mum and I'm not sure which is worse. This means I have to continue to watch and take control of the boat. I know how to work it now, but I'm aching with weariness, as I can't rest for too long. Luckily, it's not too difficult as long as the storms stay away and the night skies remain bright. If this carries on, we should still be able to stay on track.

Dad's tucked inside the cabin. I made him lie down, wrapped in both the cloak and the blanket. I could hear the rattle of his breath. I know each intake of breath is a struggle for him. He grips my hand briefly. "I must watch for the Ravangers."

"I can watch, Dad, don't worry, and it's still light."

"As soon as the darkness comes, so do they. They're the rats of the sea," he coughs. "Be alert, Jack. We can't afford to – " His coughs take over, shaking his frail body. I wrap him up tighter and hush him until his eyes slowly close.

On the bed, Jenna watches me with her dark eyes. Her face is half in shadow. "Is it The Plague, Jack? Has it come for Dad?"

"He's just tired, that's all." I show her my brightest smile, though it feels tight and false. "He'll be better soon."

I will not let him die. Not today. Not any day.

I watch the sea with a calm kind of sadness. The water rolls on, grey and endless, and after days, weeks and months of the same sight it begins to blur into murky nothingness.

The sea is such a strange thing. We have

had to live our lives with it around us for so long. Once it was a protection and our means of survival – but then it turned against us and became our biggest enemy. Humans learnt to fear it – the rising waves and sweeping seas – watching as it crashed over countries and lands, swallowing everything in its path. And then, over time, we learnt to adapt again – to see the water as an ally, something to respect and cherish. It's part of us now.

A gull sweeps past me, cawing loudly. I'm

sure it's the same gull that's followed the boat for the past few days.

"Hey!" I cry out to him, watching as it swoops and dips into the water. "Hey! Bird. Look at me! Look, I'm here!"

I wave at it, at this skinny, grey-feathered creature. It's the first living thing outside this boat that I've seen for days. Our fishing nets have been empty for too long.

"I know you're hungry. I am too. Where are the fish, eh? Why can't we catch any?"

The gull lifts its wings and flies above my head. It's looking for food too and it'll be disappointed. We have so little now and what we do have, we need to preserve.

"Hey!"

The gull swoops across the boat, calling. Its cry is tired and strained.

"Have you seen the mountains, bird?" I say back. "Am I going the right way?"

No reply; it circles the boat again, slightly higher now.

"Have you seen the mountains?" I repeat desperately. "What are they like? Are the people nice? Are they well?"

The bird simply squalls again and tears away in a burst of feather and bone.

I am alone once again.

Day spills into evening, which is the very worst time of all. The coldness sweeps across us and even the boat seems to shiver in the night breeze. I'm glad that Jenna and Dad are tucked up inside the cabin, but even there they'll not be protected from the chilly draughts and icy air.

When Dad was well, he would base himself on the deck, keeping watch, draped in blankets, whilst we tried to sleep in the cabin. Then I would take over in the daytime. It worked for a long time and meant that we both got enough rest. However, those cold nights, along with lashing ice rain is what I think led to Dad's sickness; at least I hope it's that and not The Plague.

Now I'm steering the ship day and night and only grabbing snatches of rest at the peak of the day, when the sea is at its calmest and there's less risk of being caught unexpectedly by a Ravanger boat.

It's hard to focus now. My eyes are tired and my body aches. I'm also so hungry that my stomach feels swollen and hard inside me. We ate tomatoes from the jar today, alongside some dry biscuits that had lost all their taste. Dad refused to eat at all, but selfishly it meant there was more for me and Jenna.

I groan and stretch, trying to keep my eyes fixed on the horizon. Dad's taught me to always stay alert. To be on guard. The Ravangers have boats that are bigger and faster; they can creep up on you before you notice – like a cat that's about to strike a mouse. Dad's told me the stories. No boat survives a Ravanger attack, least of all anyone on a tiny battered old boat like ours.

I can't think about this now. The worry makes my chest hurt. It's difficult to breathe.

I look up at the stars instead, focusing on their welcoming brightness. Dad loves the stars. He told me they are our guiding lights. They will show us the right way to go. He showed me all the constellations he knew – the Great Bear, Orion, Lyra …

"There's comfort in knowing these stars have been here long before us, and they'll be there after us too," he said gently, his hand on my shoulder. "They're like the knowing eyes of the sky, watching over us. They've seen it all. And wherever we are in the world, these same stars will be winking back at us."

I smile sadly as I remember his words. "No matter how faraway we are, we still share the sea and sky."

At first, I'm not sure what I'm seeing. The sky and the sea merge into one in the dark. The twinkling light in the distance could easily be another star.

I blink and take a deep breath, swallowing cold salty air.

The blinking light is slowly moving. That glowing light is getting bigger.

It's not a star. It can't be.

It's another boat.

I swallow again. The taste is now bitter in my throat.

Ravangers.

Chapter 4

We survived the night.

I spent most of it on the deck, staring out at the lights – hoping that they weren't advancing at any great speed in our direction. It was hard to tell, especially when sleep tugged at my eyes, and my legs urged for my body to curl up somewhere warm. I convinced myself that it might be another small boat like ours, looking for shelter, or a fishing boat searching for food. There was no reason to believe it was anything deadly.

Except, Dad had warned me long ago that not many boats existed now, so many had been damaged during the Storm Years. Most people had to build their own out of whatever material they could find but they were unlikely to last long in the rough waters, nor were they likely to have anything fancy like solar-powered lights included. The Ravangers made sure they took the best boats that survived and built their new life on the seas, sailing from place to place and causing chaos. We were lucky that Grandad was a fisherman and that he'd stored his boat safely up high long before many others did.

This boat and all that's inside of it is all we have left.

In those long, dark hours, there were times when I imagined the lights were dancing, almost taunting me. Other times, I wondered if I could see them at all.

Suddenly, I saw the looming ship of the Ravangers approaching, its stern facing ours, and shadowy figures standing on board ready to capture us. It was only when I wobbled on the spot and almost fell, that I realised I had fallen asleep briefly on watch. In reality, the lights hadn't seemed to move at all.

By first light, I couldn't see anything, and I chose that time to creep into the cabin and get some rest. I knew I could only afford an hour or two but that was enough and being pressed up against Jenna and listening to her soft snores was enough to comfort me.

The other boat must have moved away. We were safe, for now.

I've checked the nets and there are a few fish caught inside. Only tiny ones, but that doesn't matter. It's food. I take the fish and the strands of seaweed caught around them and prepare us a simple breakfast.

Jenna's excited and eats hers quickly. I worry that she doesn't get enough good food. We have some dried fruit left that I keep aside for her each day. Her face is thin and gaunt, and her dark hair is flat and dull. She looks thin enough to snap into two.

I try and feed Dad a little too, although he is groaning and fighting against me. His skin is hot to the touch. I've scattered some healing herbs into his dish; we don't have much left but I'm hoping it will be enough to break his fever.

"Jack … The Ravangers?" His voice is barely a rasp. "Did they come?"

"I don't think so, Dad," I say calmly. I don't tell him about the lights. It was probably nothing and I don't want him to work himself up for nothing.

He shakes his head. "These open seas have been quiet for too long ... They'll be close. I can sense it."

"We must be close to the mountains now, Dad," I say brightly, mopping his brow with cool water. "This won't be for much longer."

"If my maps are right, we are ... but the maps were plotted from the times before the floods. It's hard to be sure – " His brow creases. "Keep following the stars, Jack. We should be there – " His eyelids close and a sigh rattles through his chest.

I stroke his hand carefully. "It's OK, Dad. I'll keep following the stars," I tell him. "We'll find our new home soon."

Jenna sits next to me on the deck. It's cold but bright. I think we're at the edge of winter now. The sky is heavy above us. I'm trying to ignore the sight and shape of the clouds that roll across. We won't survive another storm.

"Tell me about Mum," Jenna urges. "Tell me that story again."

Jenna likes me talking about Mum, even though my memories are getting cloudy and broken, like a picture drawn in pencil that's started to be erased. I can still just about see her face. She was tall and pretty, with long dark hair very similar to Jenna's and a bright, wide smile.

"She was important to the community," I say. "She was a healer. She knew how to fix wounds, and which herbs could help with certain things, and she was the one who used to bring new babies into the world. She learnt it from her mum before her. Everyone came to her when they got sick."

"Did everyone come to her when The Plague came?"

I nod. "Mum didn't know what it was, but she heard talk from other villagers of this sickness that was killing so many. People would have a fever, then their bodies would swell and very often they died quite quickly. There wasn't much she could do except make them comfortable."

"And that's how she got sick? She caught it from them?"

"No – " I pause. It was hard talking about Mum. It always made me sad. "I mean, yes – she did catch it, or something like it, but then she got better."

"But Dad always said that she died." Jenna looks confused. "When I ask him about it, he gets upset and won't tell me. I know he thinks I'm too little, but I'm not. I'm really not."

Jenna has a sulky look on her face that she pulls when she really wants something. It always makes me smile.

"Mum got hurt after she got better. There were people in the village who were angry that she survived. People asked why she did, when so many didn't."

I don't tell Jenna the names they called her. They accused her of keeping herbs and potions to herself. There was a big argument and Mum was pushed and pulled about.

Dad didn't tell me many details after that. Only that he saw her being carried off by strangers. When Dad tried to find her, he was told she'd died. The guilt of not being there to protect her nearly destroyed him.

"So those people hurt her?" Jenna frowns. "And that was it? She was gone?"

My heart feels so heavy. I sigh. "I don't know why they did it. She could have helped so many. There weren't many people left in the village and then a boat came, from the mountains. They told Dad about the new community they'd set up there, how they were looking for people to come and join them. People with skills and a good heart. But Dad couldn't go, not then anyway."

Instead, he spent months trying to find out what happened to Mum and getting no answers.

In the end, things became more desperate. The Plague was spreading fast, and our village was badly affected. Dad had been given a map of the seas by the visitors from before. They asked him to follow on when he was ready. So, he fixed up Grandad's old fishing boat and told us one cold dark night that we would be leaving.

Leaving the memory of Mum.

Leaving Elise.

And leaving everything we knew and loved behind.

The wind is picking up. I look up at the skies and the sight sends a chill deep into my bones. The darkness is a sign that a storm is on the way. I start to hurry Jenna into the cabin and as I do, the first drops of rain start to fall – fast and fat against the wood.

"Come on," I urge. "We need to shelter."

Even now, storms are our biggest fear. The boat is old and small and may not be able to hold up against strong winds and rain. Also, we fear that each storm that comes may be the start of another unending one, where more floods would be caused.

We fear the sky and we fear the sea.

This is our life now.

Chapter 5

The storm is a bad one. It's strong and relentless and thrusts against us as we hide in the cabin, wobbling our tiny door and frail windows, longing to get in and claim us. The boat rocks from side to side, tipping uselessly in the wind's cruel grasp. I close my eyes, terrified that each gust will send a wave crashing over that will tip us into the sea.

There's nothing we can do. It's a waiting game.

Jenna crouches on the floor, by the bed, singing softly to Lola. I smile at how brave she is.

I turn my attention to Dad. His fever is still high and he's still asleep, muttering occasionally under his breath. His eyelids flutter as if he's having dreams.

I encourage him to drink water, with some of our remaining herbs added. I want to tell him how worried I am. I have no idea where we are, and the store cupboard is almost bare. Even if I'm really careful with rations, we probably only have food to last us a week, and water to last a week more. If we don't catch any more fish, we'll starve out here.

That's if the storm doesn't finish us off first.

The wind howls as if in agreement with me and the boat groans and creaks under its pressure. Another gust sends us tipping to one side; I end up hitting the side of the table and hurting my ribs in the process. Dad is thrown across the floor and moans in pain. Jenna clutches the side of the bed.

I stumble over to Jenna and hold her against me. My side is throbbing, and my stomach is unsettled from all the movement of the boat. I feel sick.

"Hold on," I whisper to her. "Just hold on. It'll be over soon. I promise."

We wait, the three of us, as our boat tosses us about. We are like fish trapped in a net. And all the while the wind is an endless roar outside.

I'm not sure how long it takes to pass. All I do know is I'm sick at least twice, and all of us are covered in bruises by the time the boat begins to still.

As the boat begins to steady, I feed us cold chicken soup and risk using some of the peaches that we have stored in jars. I drain the juice on to Dad's lips, and hope that the vitamins and goodness will help him. Now he's barely making a sound and I know this is a very bad sign.

"You can't leave us, Dad," I whisper. "I can't do this on my own."

Tears blur my eyes. I have no idea how damaged the boat is and if the storm has moved us off route from the mountains. All I know is that it's getting much harder to fight the desperate feeling that's building up inside me.

Once we've eaten and the winds have eased, I step outside to inspect the boat. Darkness is falling, so I use the wind-up torch to look around. I notice that one of the sails is badly torn and is flapping sadly in the remaining breeze. Thankfully, the other is still intact.

Amazingly, the rest of the boat looks to be in good order. Dad always told me what a good shipbuilder Grandad had been, and I guess this is the absolute proof that he was. I feel myself begin to relax a little.

The air smells fresh and clean, like it always does after a storm and there's a sharpness there, the tang of the salt which is much stronger now. I'll have to check the nets in the morning; I just hope they haven't been ripped away.

It's calmer now and I should be too, but as I stare out at the horizon, I see those lights again, blinking in the distance; I don't think it's my imagination but those lights seem to be a bit bigger.

It's getting closer.

Chapter 6

"Tell me about Dad again."

Jenna's curled up on the deck next to me; Lola is on her lap. I've wrapped the blanket around us both so I can watch the sea. It's hard to stay awake, but Jenna's constant wriggling and asking questions help with that.

"Dad?" I frown. "What do you mean – before?"

"Yes," she nods keenly. "You told me he was important. Why?"

I smile. I like this story. It's one I can remember best, growing up with a dad who was strong and in charge, a dad who was going to make everything better.

In our village, Dad was one of the leaders. He always told me he didn't want this title, but it kind of fell to him, probably because of his dad – our grandad – who'd been so important during the Storm Years. Grandad's house had been on the highest point in the village. He'd taken many people in and used his boat to find food and resources. He'd been kind and fearless and, when he died, Dad took over the role.

Dad told me that it could be hard sometimes, living in a small community. It was difficult to keep everyone happy and working together. People still spoke of the old times, when the land hadn't been half covered by the sea. There was a great deal of sadness and fear.

Dad and some others helped to restore faith and hope. The village began to thrive and, when Dad met my mum, they became a respected couple.

And then The Plague came, and everything changed.

"Dad was well respected," I tell Jenna. "He was kind and strong and everyone listened to him."

Later, he would fix up Grandad's boat even more by adding extra sails and reinforcing the cabin. It would be our new home, our escape. Dad was the one in charge. He looked after us.

"The mountains will be different," I tell Jenna. "This will all be worth it. It has to be."

I still remember the day I called for Elise. It was spring. We'd planned to spend the day by the river, fishing and swimming in the cool waters. I loved spending time with her. She was funny and adventurous and brave. She didn't care about getting muddy or wet. She just liked to laugh.

That day was different though. I could tell as soon as I knocked on the door. Her mum answered and her face was deathly grey. She couldn't look at me.

"I've come to get Elise."

"You can't." She shook her head. "I'm sorry, Jack." Her voice broke and she swiped at her eyes.

I could feel my heart thudding hard in my chest, my breath was tight in my throat, but I couldn't allow myself to believe what I knew to be true.

"But we've made plans," I argued hopelessly. "We won't be out long."

"Oh, Jack – "

I dared to look past her, at the bed made up in the tiny living room of Elise's ramshackle cottage. I saw her curled up small on the straw mattress.

Her face and neck were swollen red and her skin looked wet with sweat. She coughed and I could hear the rattle deep in her chest, like pebbles being shaken in a bucket.

"I – I only saw her two days ago," I said, my eyes unable to leave the sight of her.

Elise couldn't get sick. She was my friend. We'd known each other since we were tiny. She'd always been there for me and me for her. And yet now, I knew there was nothing I could do.

"You should go, Jack," her mum warned. "Just being here is a risk. You know that."

The Plague was so contagious; it moved from person to person so quickly. Once someone showed symptoms, we all knew it was safest to stay away. I may have already taken too many risks.

Her mum laid a hand on my shoulder as I left; I could feel her shaking.

"She always liked you, Jack," she whispered sadly.

Those words didn't make me feel any better.

I'm up at the deck, watching the horizon, waiting to see if I can make out the lights in the distance. The sky is heavy and tired after the storm and the sea still swirls and rocks in an unsettled way beneath us. I glance up at the ripped sail and hope that this is the only time they'll be damaged.

I don't think we can manage with anything more. The truth is, I don't even know how much this damage will cost us; I am no expert. I didn't take much notice when Dad showed me things to do with the boat. I thought it was boring and was too interested in other things – fun things. Now, I stand here wishing that the younger me had listened more, had asked more questions.

The only person who has the answers is Dad and he can't help me now.

As if on cue, Dad's screams suddenly pierce through the cabin. I slip and slide on the remaining puddles on the deck as I rush towards him. It feels like time is slowing, that I'm taking too long to get to him.

"Dad!" I burst through the door. Jenna's on the floor beside him. I can tell by her face that she is holding in her tears. She jumps up and rushes towards me.

"He won't stop screaming. I can't stop him, Jack. What's wrong?"

I hurry to his side and grip his hand. He's thrashing from side to side, sweat pouring down his face. The screams stop as I squeeze his hand. "It's OK, Dad, I'm here."

"Jack … Jack – " He opens his eyes; they are wide with panic. "Jack … What's happening. Where are we?"

"We're near, Dad. We'll be there soon."

The lie falls easily from my lips. What else can I say? I need to calm him, to keep him content. I also want to believe that we're still moving in the right direction, and the storm hasn't taken us off course.

"You're a good boy, Jack," he whispers.

His eyes flutter closed again. His breath, although still ragged, seems to settle. I squeeze his hand and fight back the tears.

"Will he be OK?" Jenna asks.

"Yes, of course," I reply.

Another lie. How can I be sure? I'm getting so

used to saying what I think people want to hear.

"He was calling for Mum," Jenna says softly. "I think he misses her."

I tuck Dad's blankets gently around him and brush a kiss against his hot, flushed cheek.

"I know," I say sadly. "I know."

Much later, I stand at the edge of the boat staring out. I try not to let the hopelessness overcome me. I want the night breeze to whip away my fears and to make me strong again.

I want something to show me the way.

My eyes fix on the horizon.

The lights are still there, blinking away at me – much bigger and brighter than before.

They're coming.

Chapter 7

I wake up to Dad screaming again. I've fallen asleep on the deck and am almost frozen with cold; it takes a moment or two for me to move. I almost don't want to, it's as if my limbs are glued to the wooden boards.

"Ravangers!" Dad's yelling. He's sitting up in the bed, his hair slicked back wet against his face, his eyes wide and stary. "Ravangers are coming. I can smell them. I can sense them."

Jenna peers down from the top bunk, clutching Lola. "Are they coming, Jack?"

I fight back a shiver, thinking of those bright lights. "No – no, there's no one out there."

Dad turns, his eyes are wild. "They'll come sniffing, looking for anything they can take. They'll set fire to the boat when they are done."

Jenna starts to sob softly, and I pull her into my arms.

"It's OK, Jenn, Dad's ill. He doesn't mean what he says."

"I'm scared of the Ravangers, Jack."

"I know, I know." I soothe her.

Dad's laid back down again; exhaustion has overcome him. He shivers violently on the bed, his pale eyes staring up at the ceiling. I try to ignore how grey his skin is, how frail and skinny he has become.

But there's no swelling. That has to be a good sign, right? There's no sign of The Plague.

Dad's stories about the Ravangers used to make me feel excited.

"They were like us before," Dad said. "They were villagers like us, searching for food and shelter but instead of working for a better community, they set off on their own; they decided to take from others – to steal and rob. To make us scared of them."

Dad talked of the pirates that lived years and years before that. The Ravangers were like them, using the open water as their home and picking off weaker boats as if they were food to be consumed.

"Have you ever seen one?" I asked Dad.

"They came to the village once. A great group of them. It would have been when you were a baby, Jack. We fought them off as best we could, but they still took food. They stole a boat. I was only able to keep your grandad's boat safe because we had people guarding it; after all, it was the best in the village. We were lucky that time. I never expected them to return. We knew they preferred life at sea."

Back in the village, the Ravangers were just part

of the storytelling. They were the baddies, but I didn't really worry about them. They were a faraway problem. Something I would never expect to encounter.

Now it's all I can think about.

I urge the boat to go faster, pleading and beating against the boards as if it will have any effect. I continue to hope that we're still heading in the right direction, that any moment the mountains will be in front of us – and we'll be home.

A new home.

I reach in my pocket and draw out the crumpled letter. The edges are torn and the paper itself is starting to wear. It's one of the most precious things I have left.

I don't have to open it to know what the words say. I still remember the morning Elise's mum came to me. She gave me the note with a shaky hand. "Elise told me what to write. Even though every breath hurts her, she wanted you to know."

I blink away the tears now, remembering.

Jack

I'm sorry. I heard you the other day. I wish I'd been well enough to say hello.

I miss you.

Please don't come again. Get away from here as soon as you can.

I'll never forget what a true friend you were to me.

Elise

I did go back that last night to say goodbye, but she was too ill to recognise me, and I couldn't risk the sickness to stay long.

But I regret not thanking her back.

I regret not thanking her for being the best friend I'd ever had.

Chapter 8

I dreamt of Mum.

Sleep was my escape. I slipped away to a better place. To a time when I was in Mum's arms. I could smell her, could touch her soft skin, her dark hair brushed my face as she leant over to kiss my cheek.

"It won't be long now, Jack. You'll soon be there."

"Do you promise?" I asked.

She grinned. I'd forgotten how beautiful her smile was. "Of course. You just need to hold tight. Look after your dad; make sure he drinks enough water."

"But I'm scared, Mum."

She kissed my cheek; it was as light as a breath.

"Don't lose hope, Jack. I'm with you."

I woke with a start. I was crying and all I wanted to do was be back with her, be back in her arms.

I didn't want to be here any more.

We're running out of food. Breakfast is a strange mix of beans in a jar and a few dry biscuits. Jenna doesn't want to eat. She says her tummy hurts. Dad's sleeping and I'm unable to rouse him. I eat some of the food and leave the rest for later. It tastes like sawdust and feels like it's sticking in my throat.

I'm eating simply to survive now.

"I don't want to be here any more," Jenna moans. She lies on the bed and refuses to move. "I want to go back."

"Going back would take too long. We're nearer to the mountains than we are to our village," I say, trying to stay calm. "And there's nothing left for us back there. Nothing at all."

"I don't care. I hate it and so does Lola."

I sit next to Jenna. I take her hand in mine and grip it tight. "We're going on an adventure. We're going to find people like us, new friends, and it might be scary but we need to be brave."

"OK," she whispers, her eyes shining. "I'll try."

That is all I need to hear.

The day is bright and surprisingly warm, despite the fact we're nearing winter. For a moment, my eyes are drawn to the water; is that a shoal of fish I can see? I blink, hardly able to believe it. I can see their beautiful, shimmering bodies moving just under the surface.

I blink again and they're gone.

It's just the light, that's all. The light is playing tricks on me.

I check the nets again. One was ripped too badly in the storm, but the other is still intact.

Today we've caught one small fish. It'll be enough for me to cook for tea. Hope flickers once again.

I think of Elise, and how we used to warm the fish we'd caught on small fires. Elise was always better at fishing than me. She was better at building fires too. She was pretty good at most things really.

I wonder why she caught The Plague and I didn't. We were always together, so I should've too. Dad once told me he believed some people were immune and that's why Mum hadn't been badly ill with it.

All I knew was that it wasn't fair. Elise never should've caught it.

She was too adventurous, too clever, too brave to die like that.

The fish tastes good.

Jenna eats most of it. She sits holding Dad's hand and singing to him softly under her breath.

"He likes my singing," she says. "I want to make him better."

I glance at Dad and I'm sure I can see a trace of a smile on his grey face. He seems more settled. There's been no shouting today.

"I want to be brave like you, Jack," she says.

"I'm not brave."

"Yes, you are, you're the bravest person I know," she says firmly. "And I want to be just like you. I want to help."

I smile down at my sister. Her eyes are bright, and her expression is stern. I know she means every word.

I sweep her into a hug and hold her tight. I never want to let her go.

Chapter 9

I study the charts that Dad has tacked to the cabin wall. They make little sense to me and once again I wish I'd listened when he'd first tried to explain them to me. It'd been so easy before. I'd always assumed that Dad would be beside me all the way and I would never have to fend for myself. Now, all I want to do is turn back the clock and try to remember the things he taught me.

"These maps have been written by those that ventured the seas long before us," he'd told me. "After the floods, the world changed. Countries were swallowed up and the seas joined. It's taken a long time to work out what's still out there and how it can be reached."

I trace the marks on the paper, which have faded with time and wear. The compass beside me tells me we're still heading in the right direction.

It's only a matter of days until we reach the mountains.

Or at least, I desperately hope so.

The nets have been kind to us today; there are several fish caught within them and two are fat and juicy. I place them all in a bucket, trying to fight back my excitement.

The gull swoops up above me. I'm sure it's the same one as before. Its wings are just as shaggy and frail looking, and its call sounds the same. Surely this is a good sign? Gulls are usually close to land.

"I have enough food for a day or so," I tell it proudly. "The sea is rewarding me."

The gull flies close, its beady eyes on the bucket. Its call is more broken this morning.

"Are you hungry too?" I stare up at it. "Where's your family? Where are you going?"

I must look ridiculous talking to a bird. I know a seagull can't understand me. Yet, there's something about the way it turns and flies close to my head again that makes me shudder.

It's trying to tell me something.

"Elise always loved birds," I say quietly, watching it circle the air above me. "She always said they were cleverer than you think but if you see one come close to a human, it's often a bird in need. They want something."

The gull shrieks again as if in reply.

I reach in the bucket and pull out one of the fishes, not the fattest one, but not the smallest either. I pull off its head and hold it up above my head. The bird swoops down towards it – a blur of feather and beak.

It takes off in flight with the fish head still trapped in its mouth, its dark eye meeting mine.

I'm sure it was thanking me.

Maybe I'm just seeing things.

I cook another good meal. Fish and some pickles. I even risk sharing out the last of the peaches. Jenna and I guzzle on the juice greedily. It's the best thing we've had for ages.

Dad eats a little too. He sits up, propped up on a pillow. He still has a slight fever, but he's definitely more relaxed.

"As soon as we land, we can make our new start," he tells us both. His voice still croaks, and he coughs occasionally, but it's good to hear the calmness in his words.

"Will we have a house again, Dad?" Jenna asks. "Will I have a garden like before?"

"I hope so." He frowns a little. "I'm not sure what's there, but I've been told it's safe and that's all we need for now."

Safe. I like the sound of that word. I want to wrap it around me like a blanket.

Dad insists that he can keep watch so that I can get a little rest. I'm not sure that he's ready, but I'm so tired that I agree.

I clamber on the bed beside Jenna and close my eyes. I don't plan to sleep for long. The weather's still warm and bright on the deck so I know Dad will be OK for a short while, but I don't want to risk him out there too long. I insisted he took a blanket, so Jenna and I only have one to share. Luckily, our body heat helps to keep us warm.

Sleep greets me easily and, for the first time in days, it's deep and I dream again.

I dream of Mum laughing and dancing with Dad around a campfire, her hair lit up by the brightness of the moon. I dream of Dad working on the boat, singing softly under his breath as he hammers in nails and smooths down the wood. I dream of Elise, rising from her sick bed – well and happy, waving at me and laughing.

"See Jack – it was just a trick. I wasn't poorly really. I'm better now. I'm here."

And I dream of a place faraway that's warmed by lights and scented by rich food and plants.

I dream of safety.

I wake to a bump. The ship has rocked slightly. As if it's touched something.

My heart hammers in my chest and I jump up. Are we here? Have we arrived?

I rush out of the cabin. It's still dark and it takes a while for my eyes to adjust to the shapes around me.

Dad's slumped against the door of the cabin, sleeping. I touch his head instinctively. It's warm, not blazing, but I still left him out here too long. He wasn't ready for the cold yet.

Then I lift my eyes and scan the dark sea in front of me.

Except I can't see it. Something's blocking the view.

It takes me a second or two to work out what's happened and, when I do, my breath stops in my throat.

The other boat is right alongside us.

Chapter 10

The boat casts a long shadow over us, like a monster from the sea. I can't move. All I can do is stare up at the huge thing – twice the size of our pathetic craft and groaning as it sits alongside us, as if waiting to attack.

I can't make out any movement – but it's so dark. The Ravangers might be creeping low to keep themselves unnoticed.

I swallow and try and steady my breath. I can't afford to stand here frozen. These people will come at any moment and pluck me off the boat like I'm some kind of annoying insect. They will probably toss me into the cold sea. I have to protect Dad and Jenna and I don't have much time.

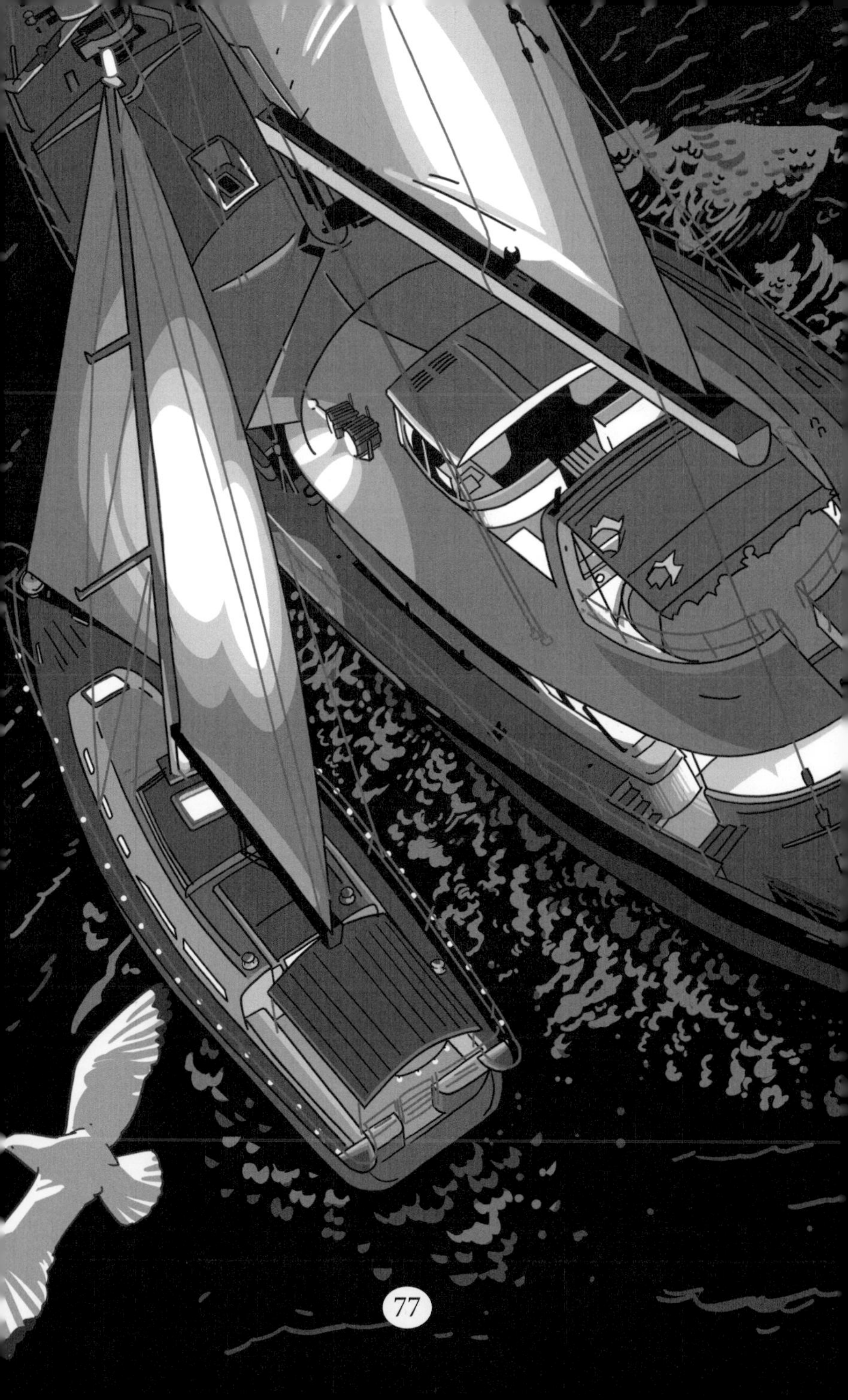

I try to wake Dad, but he's sleeping deeply. I can hear the rattle is back in his chest and it doesn't sound good. I'm not even sure what to do. I nudge him, but he's back in a fever-rich sleep.

He's hidden in the shadows though, tucked into the small corner by the door to the cabin. I pull the blanket over him further. Maybe here he won't be noticed. Not at first at least. He's just a shape in the dark.

I run into the cabin.

Jenna is curled up on the top bunk. I wake her up gently. "Jenna. Jenn," I hiss. "I need you to come with me."

"What? I'm sleeping … Leave me alone."

"Jenn. It's important." I pull her up. "I need you to hide."

I feel her stiffen. "Why?"

"I think there's another boat here. We don't have much time."

"The Ravangers?" Her voice rises a bit. "What

about Dad?"

"Leave Dad to me. I'll look after him, but I need you to help me," I plead. "I need you to hide."

She nods. "Where?"

I look around the cabin. There aren't many places. There's a small built-in cupboard where we go to the toilet, but that would be too obvious. In the food store, there's a large barrel; it was once full of water, but now we're running low.

"Come," I say. "Quickly."

I tug the lid off the barrel and stare down inside. It's dark and the remaining water will be cold, but I don't know what other choice we have.

"I'm going to put you in here," I say. "It won't be for long, OK? It'll be like being in a cold bath."

"I don't like cold baths."

"I know you don't, but remember you said you wanted to be brave." I pause. I think I can hear noises outside. Was that a voice? Did something just clank against our boat?

I pick her up and lift her in. She's skinny enough to fit in. She squeals as her body touches the water but then she is silent.

"I'll be back soon, I promise," I tell her. "If I take too long, tip the barrel to get out."

I leave the lid half off, so that she's not in complete darkness and so she can escape if she needs to. I can now hear footsteps on the deck outside. They're coming for me.

I really am alone.

I reach under the bed and grope around until I find it. Dad's knife. I walk out towards the deck. If they are going to try and capture me, I'll try to defend myself.

My hand is shaking. My legs feel weak. My heart is beating far too fast.

I step out.

Someone grabs my hand immediately. It's a strong grip. I look up at the shadowy figure in front of me and scream. The knife falls to the floor.

It seems I'm not much of a fighter, after all.

And then everything goes dark.

I don't know how long it is until I wake up. Everything feels swirly. My tongue is fat in my mouth and my throat is dry. I have to blink several times to make out the shapes in front of me.

I'm on the top bunk in the cabin. I can hear Dad snoring on the bed below me.

Was it all just a bad dream?

No – because I look down and I see Jenna on the floor wrapped in fresh blankets. She's drinking something hot. A man stands between us. He's dressed in black, but his face isn't scary – it's soft, an expression of concern is etched upon it.

He turns towards me and slowly offers his hand. "I'm Oscar," he says. "I'm sorry I scared you. It's just you had the knife and I – "

"Who are you? Are you a Ravanger?"

He chuckles softly. "No – no. We drove those boats away years ago. They were cowards, the lot of them. The ones that we didn't catch have disbanded and fled faraway. We don't tolerate such behaviour in our seas now."

"So, who are you?"

He smiles. "I'm part of the new community from the mountains. We check the seas regularly for small boats like yours. We know how difficult the journey can be, and we want to ensure no souls are lost along the way." He pats my arm gently. "We're here to help you. I know you're scared,

but please don't be. I don't want you hiding your little sister in water barrels any more."

I look down at Dad, who's still sleeping. "My dad – he's – "

"Sick. I know." Oscar nods. "We have someone who can help him in the mountains. She's one of the best. And we have plenty of food and drink on our boat. It'll be a far more pleasant journey for you. You just need to trust us and come with us. Can you do that?"

I hesitate, but then look at Dad again, at Jenna shivering in her blankets. What other choice do I have? I have to hope these are the people we've been looking for. I have to believe we are no longer alone.

Chapter 11

Now I am sick.

Very sick.

It's not just seasickness that plagues me. I'm ill with something else. I suspect that it's what Dad had. All those days of nursing him and now I've succumbed to it.

The fever is deep within me; I shake and shiver all the time despite having thick, deep blankets wrapped around me. My body aches despite being on a soft mattress in a cabin of my own and I can't eat despite being offered the best food I've had for months.

The people are friendly here.

Oscar visits me daily. He brings me water and puts cool cloths on my forehead. He tells me how my family are. Jenna's being looked after by one of the female crew and eating lots. Dad is recovering and has started to move around the boat. He insists on seeing me, but the crew are trying to keep me as isolated as possible – just in case my infection spreads.

"What about you?" I say to Oscar. "You could catch this."

Oscar shrugs. "I'm not going to let a brave warrior like you fight this alone. Besides, we're only days from home. If I get sick, there's someone that can help me. I can risk it because I'm strong – but your dad and Jenna are weaker. We need to protect them."

I understand. I don't want to risk harm to either of them. So instead, I sleep or stare up at the ceiling, trying to ignore the pains in my body and the weakness that consumes me. We are so close now.

Oscar tells me a little about the mountain community. He says there are thousands of people that have made their way there – some on foot, over the lands that still exist, and others by boat like us, from further away. Families that are looking for something better, a new start, fresh hope.

"It's a good place," Oscar says. "The Plague isn't there at all. We grow food. There's a good water supply. We've built new homes and even a school. We hope that life can really begin again."

"It sounds wonderful," I whisper. I'm drifting in and out of dreams. It's hard to stay with him.

"You will be an important part of it, I can tell," Oscar says. "All of you." Then he leans in and whispers in my ear. “Just hold on, Jack. Please hold on.”

Please hold on.

His whispers send me into the darkness again.

I dream I'm back on the small boat with Dad and Jenna. We're on the deck together, staring out at the view in front of us. The sea is clear. The sun lights up the sky, and we're sailing straight towards it.

Dad squeezes my hand. "I told you we'd do it, Jack," he says. "I told you we'd make it."

There's no fear at all.

We're finally free.

Chapter 12

We're here. At the mountains, but I'm too sick to feel anything at all. All I want to do is sleep.

I was carried out of the boat and then wrapped up and placed in the back of a cart. It was a long and bumpy journey, but I don't remember much of it. I kept drifting in and out of sleep. The fever is deep inside my bones now and it's harder to move, to speak or to keep my eyes open for long.

I heard Dad whisper to me, telling me that he loved me and that we were nearly there.

Sleep was a release, and I allowed it to swallow me up.

I couldn't do anything else.

I wake up. It's bright! There is lots of bustle and movement around me. A man touches my hand. "Jack – you're here. At the mountains. We're trying to get you better. Our best healer is coming."

I nod. My lips are cracked and dry and my throat is so swollen, spit pools in my mouth. I wonder if Elise felt this bad at the end.

I must have The Plague. Dad survived – I know, but this, this is worse. I'm so weak, so sick. I'm not immune. I'm like the others.

I did all of this for nothing.

I close my eyes again.

I dream of Mum. This time she's sitting with me. She strokes my damp head and places something cool on my skin. "You need to eat, Jack," she says softly. "You're wasting away."

She feeds me spoonfuls of sweet tasting broth. It's the best thing I've tasted for ages. My stomach aches for more.

"This will help," she tells me. "It has the

medicine in it that you need."

"Mum – "

My voice is a crack. I can't speak. I blink at the sight of her. She's so beautiful. Her hair is as long and dark as I remember, her kind, bright eyes are fixed on mine. She looks older.

"I've missed you so much," she whispers. "But you must fight now, Jack. Fight this, please. I need you back."

I wake up in tears. A woman I don't recognise rushes over and tries to comfort me.

"I've been having dreams," I stutter.

She touches my head. "Your fever is reduced, and you're far more alert now. Let me check with the healer."

Another woman approaches me. I know

who it is immediately, from her movement, from her posture – I'd know my mum anywhere. I start to cry all over again.

"We thought you were dead," I say.

Mum sits beside me and she strokes my head. "I know. I know – I've spoken to your dad and Jenna. He's told me everything. I'm so sorry."

Mum slowly tells me her story – how she was attacked that night and left for dead. "My head was hurt," she says quietly. "When I was found, I couldn't remember anything – only how scared I was. The people who found me were asking villagers to go with them to the mountains and they took me with them. They had a healer here; they knew they had a chance to make me better."

"And they did – " I say.

"Yes. Alek was a wonderful man. He healed me and slowly my memory came back. I wanted to get back to you, but news came that the whole village had been wiped out by The Plague. Oscar heard that a few families had escaped by boat, and I just hoped that you were among them. Oscar and his crew have been looking for families so he can bring them to safety."

I start to cry again. "I thought you were lost forever."

Mum's eyes glint with tears. "I did too but I had hope. I had to believe you'd find me." She pulls me into a hug, and I grip her so tight. I never want to lose her again.

"Will I be OK?" I whisper.

"Yes." She strokes my cheek. "Alek taught me how to be the best healer and now that he's passed, it's my job to keep everyone well. Your infection has gone; you'll be better in a few days."

"And what then?" I ask.

"Then we'll be a family again," she says, her voice wobbling. "Like I said – I never gave up hope. There's a house waiting for you, for all of us. We can be together again."

The days pass slowly, but this no longer matters to me. Mum, Dad and Jenna are by my bedside constantly. Mum and Dad hold hands and laugh together. Dad's still frail, but I can see the light in his eyes again. He's stronger already. Jenna's laughing and playing again. And though I'm still weak, I can feel my strength returning. I know I'll survive this.

A sense of normality has returned.

Mum has introduced us to others in the camp. She tells us stories of her time here. This is a good place.

I still see my seagull, swooping in the sky, and occasionally he visits me at my window.

Finally, we all have a home again.

Book talk questions

How does Jack's family cope with the challenges of living in a flooded world?

What is the significance of the mysterious ship following Jack's family?

How do the stars guide Jack on his journey?

What does Jack's journey teach him about resilience and courage?

How does the relationship between Jack and his sister change throughout the story?

What sacrifices does Jack have to make during his journey?

Would you have done anything differently to the characters?

Why is family important in the story?

What do you think Jack would have done differently if he had more help along the way?

How does the ending of the book bring closure to Jack's journey?

Ask the author

What inspired you to write *Flooded World*?

I enjoy reading books that are set in near futures and also have an interest in environmental matters. Sadly, there is a risk that the world could be a very different place in the future and it intrigues me to think how people will cope and adapt.

Do you have a favourite illustration in the book?

I love the illustrations so much that it's hard to pick a favourite. Jack standing in the doorway while Elise is so poorly is very powerful and made me want to cry.

Which character do you most identify with?

I think I most identify with Jack. He is trying to be strong and determined in a very grim situation, and that is what I have had to do sometimes in my past. He doesn't give up on his dreams, no matter how scared he is.

What's your favourite thing about being an author?

I love being able to let the ideas in my head become fully formed books. I also love hearing from readers and knowing that they have enjoyed my books.

What do you hope that readers get out of this book?

I hope that they enjoy Jack's journey and see that even in desperate times, hope can shine through.

Which part of the book was your favourite to write?

I loved writing about the Ravangers. I've always had a bit of an obsession with pirates, so it was great fun to create these characters.

What sort of skills do you think would be useful if you were in Jack's situation?

Resilience, some food/cookery skills and also some knowledge about boats! Also great story-telling skills to keep morale up.

Collins
BIG CAT

Published by Collins
An imprint of HarperCollins*Publishers*

The News Building
1 London Bridge Street
London SE1 9GF
UK

Macken House
39/40 Mayor Street Upper
Dublin 1
D01 C9W8
Ireland

10 9 8 7 6 5 4 3 2

ISBN 978-0-00-874488-5

British Library Cataloguing-in-Publication Data
A catalogue record for this publication is available from the British Library.

Author: Eve Ainsworth
Illustrator: Carl Pearce (Beehive Illustration)
Publisher: Laura White
Commissioning editor: Holly Woolnough
Development editor: Zoë Clarke
Product manager: Holly Woolnough
Content editor: Selin Akca
Copyeditor: Sally Byford
Proofreader: Catherine Dakin
Reviewer: Lisa Davis
Cover designer: Sarah Finan
Internal design: 2Hoots Publishing Services Ltd
Typesetter: Jouve India Ltd
Production controller: Katharine Willard

Collins would like to thank the teachers and children at Grange Primary School, Southwark, for being part of the development of Big Cat Read On.

Printed in the UK.